Nn Oo Pp

Qq Rr Ss

Tt Uu Vv

Ww Xx

Yy Zz

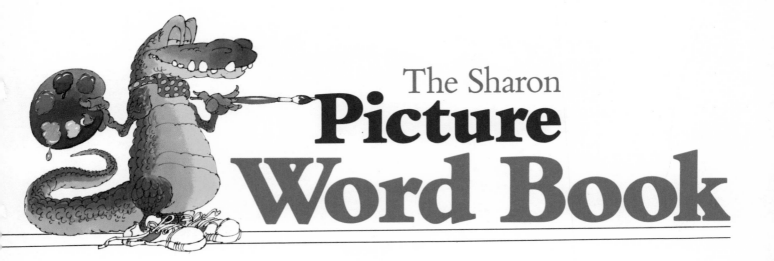

The Sharon
Picture
Word Book

All correspondence and inquiries should be directed to Sales Dept., Sharon Publications, Inc., 105 Union Avenue, Cresskill, New Jersey 07626.

Sharon Publications Inc. is an Edrei Communications Company.

ISBN #0-89531-031-7
Cover Designed by Rod Gonzalez

Printed in Singapore by Khai Wah Litho Pte Ltd

The Sharon picture Wordbook

by
Frank Daniel and Evelyne Johnson

Sharon Publications, Inc.
Cresskill, N.J. 07626

Aa

alley

alligator

alphabet

ascot

artist

daniel

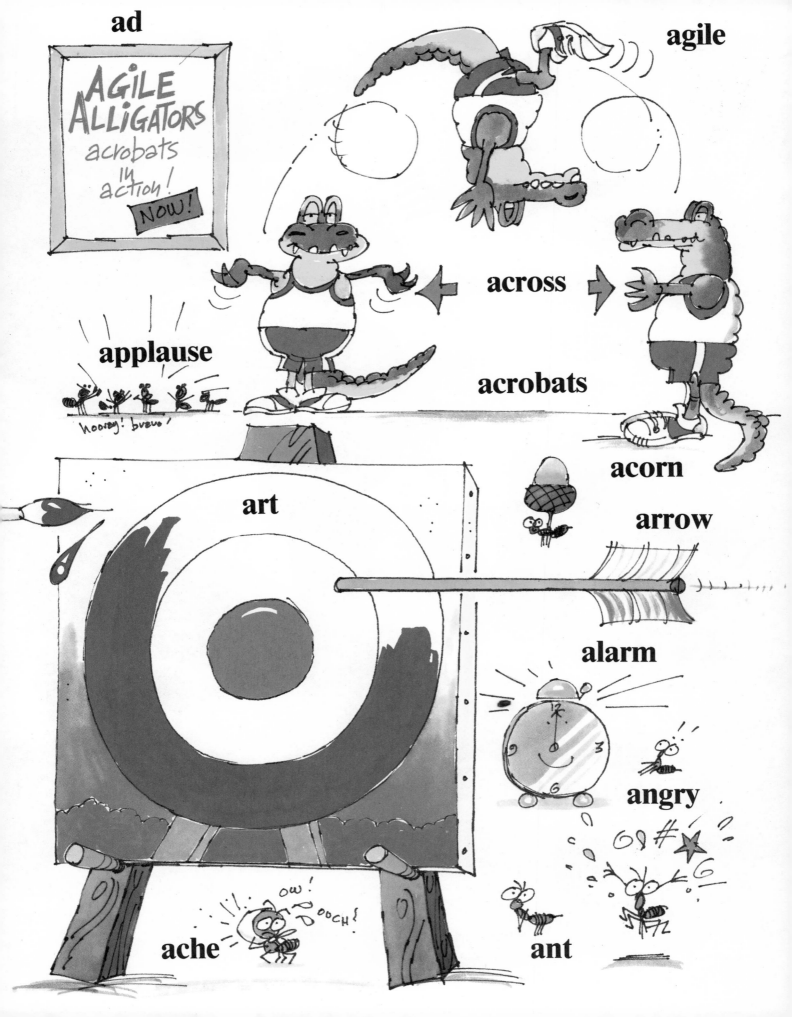

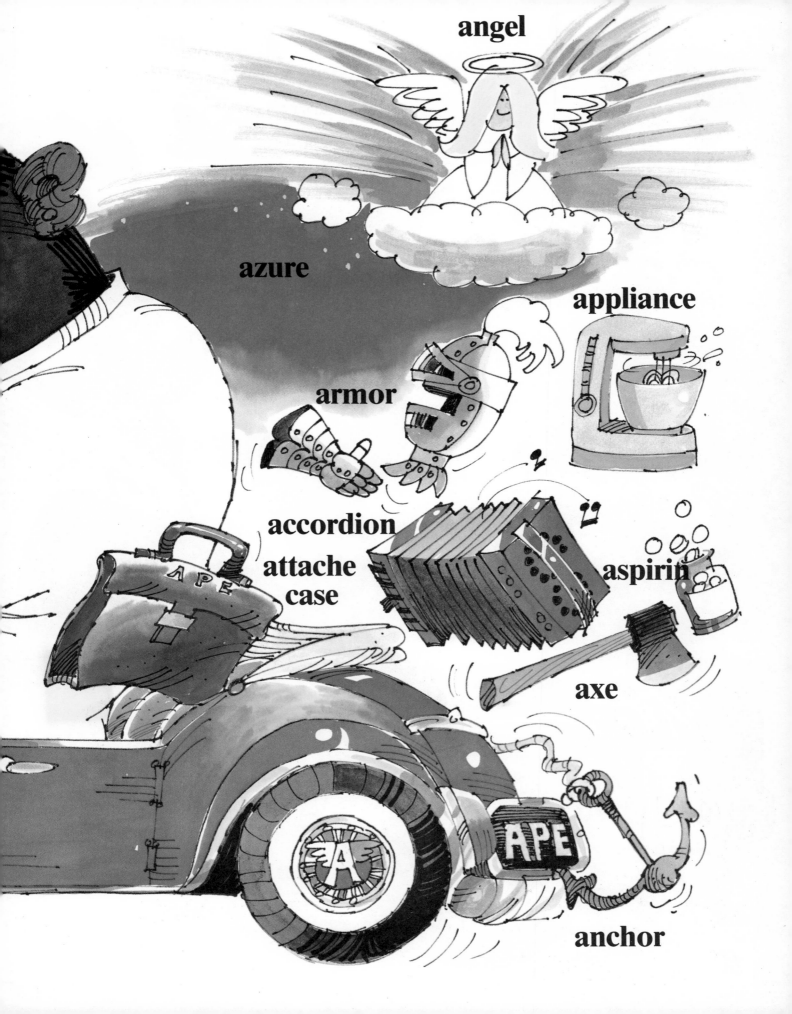

Cc

Christmas tree

curtains

cloud

chimney

cabin

cube

child

Cynthia

Carol

crimson

crayon

electric light

eye
glasses

emblem

emu

eagle

envelope

fly

forest

fin

fish

field

finch

feather

fir tree

furrow

fork

food

fir cone

fur

fertilizer

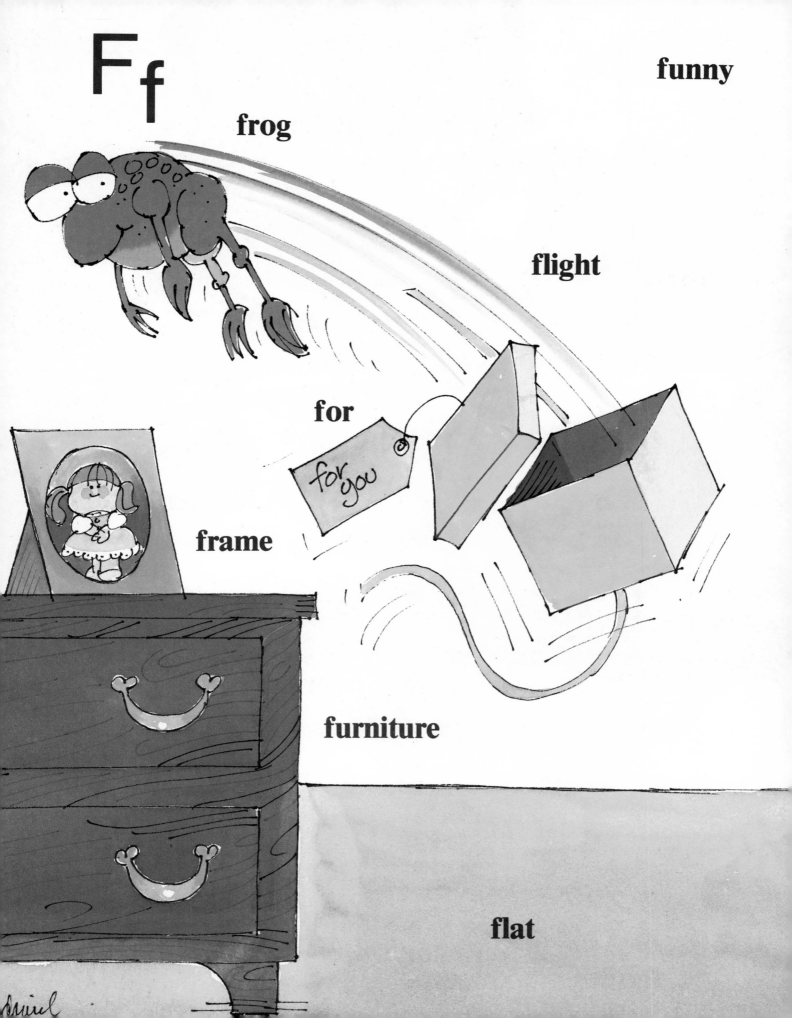

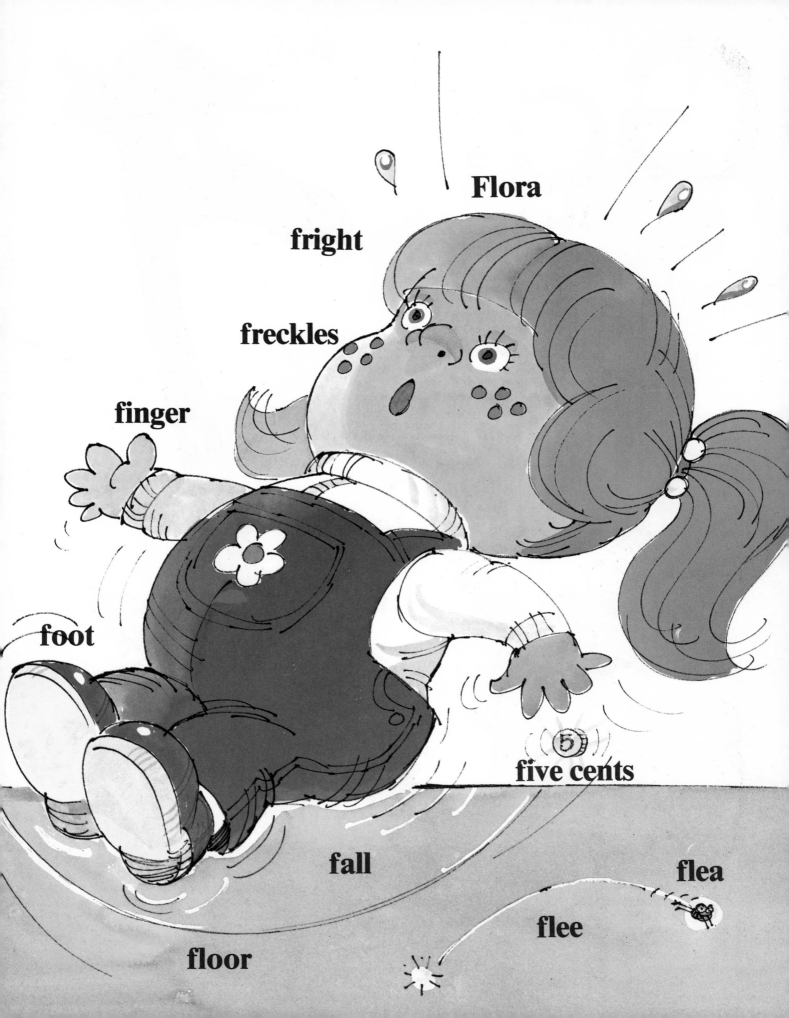

heaven

hot

highway

halloween

hat

helmet

Harry

hockey

hockey
stick

I i

Israel

Ireland

Italy

igloo

ice

idea

icicle

indent

inside

ice cream

insects

intergalactic

ivy

interview

intelligent
iris

I SUPPORT MY SCHOOL

involved

ink

I i

INDIAN
East

INDIAN
American

INTERNATIONAL

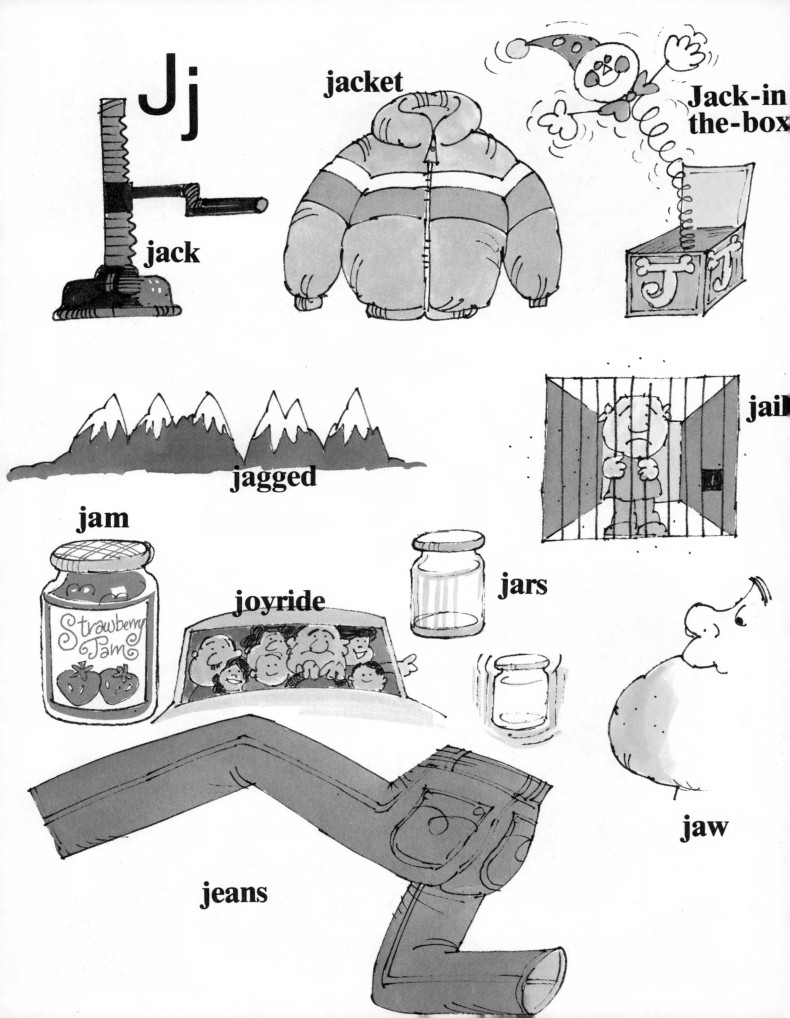

Jj

jack

jacket

Jack-in-the-box

jagged

jail

jam

joyride

jars

jaw

jeans

jeep

jeweler

jigsaw

jig
saw

job

jockey

jogger

joining

jaguar

join

jut

jeep

K k

katydid

kangaroo

knapsack

kerchief

kettle

key

knitting

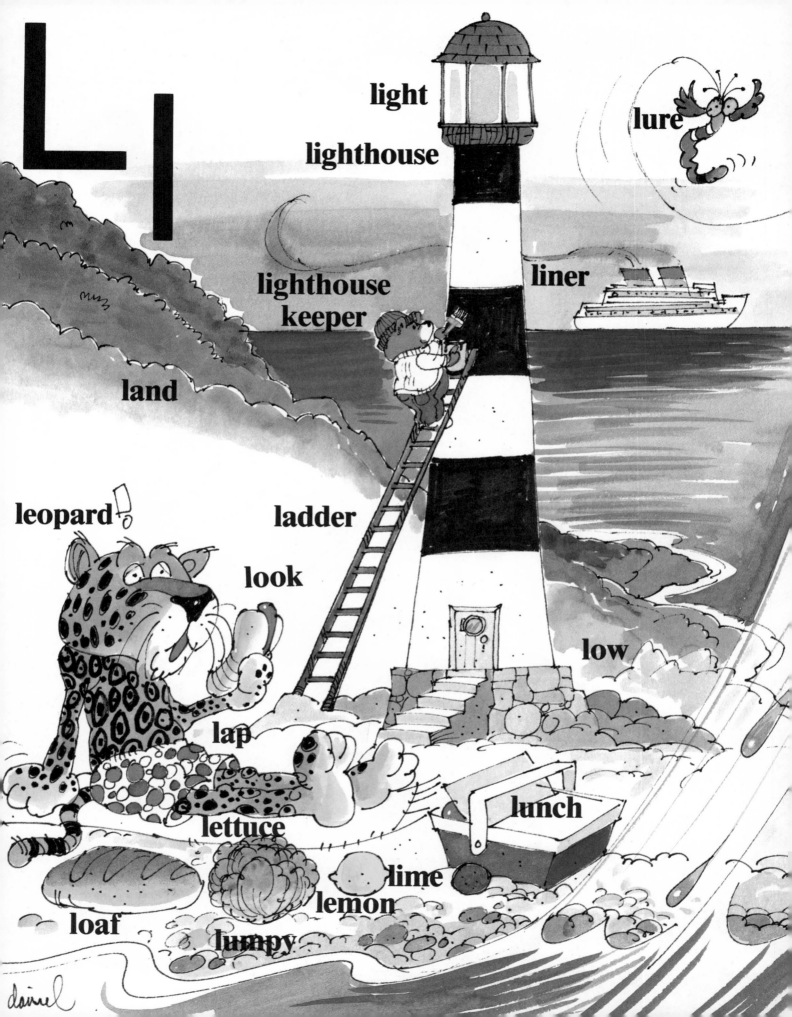

lavender

lily of the valley

look

link

linen

lace

lily

lupin

lilac

lamb

lizard

leaf

Nn

nursery school

nasturmium

net

nine

1 2 3 4 5 6 7 8 9

nickel

newt

nobody

new

neck

nut

nursery rhymes

Oo

oboe

owl

ostrich

overcoat

outlaw

oxford

overshoe

orb

over

oil

overgrown

oasis

opera

oil well

oriental

open

outlet

Oo

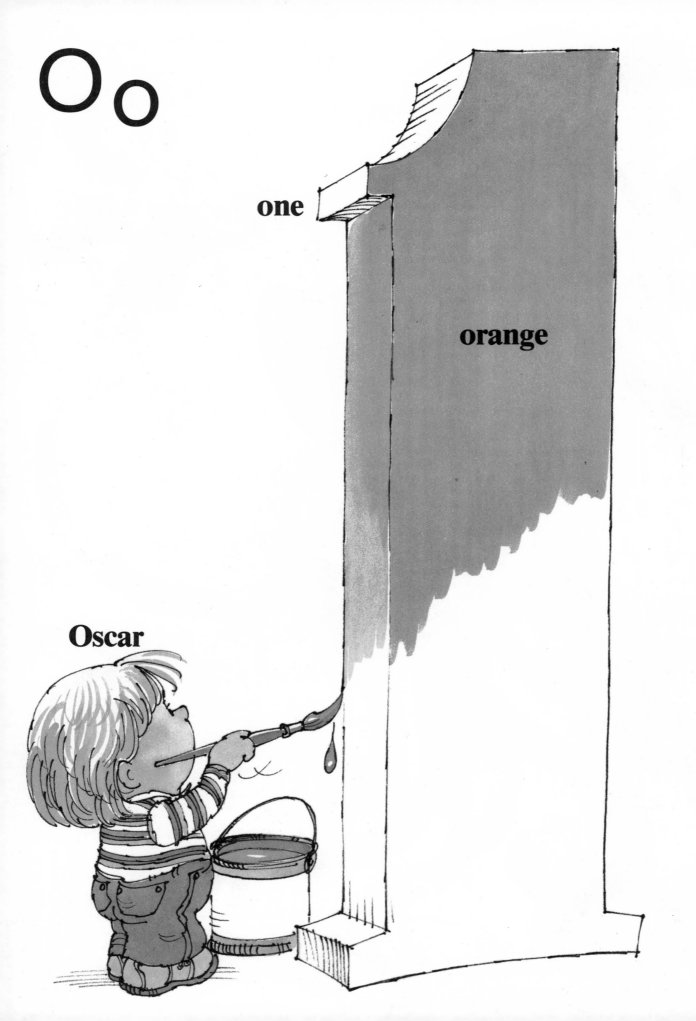

one

orange

Oscar

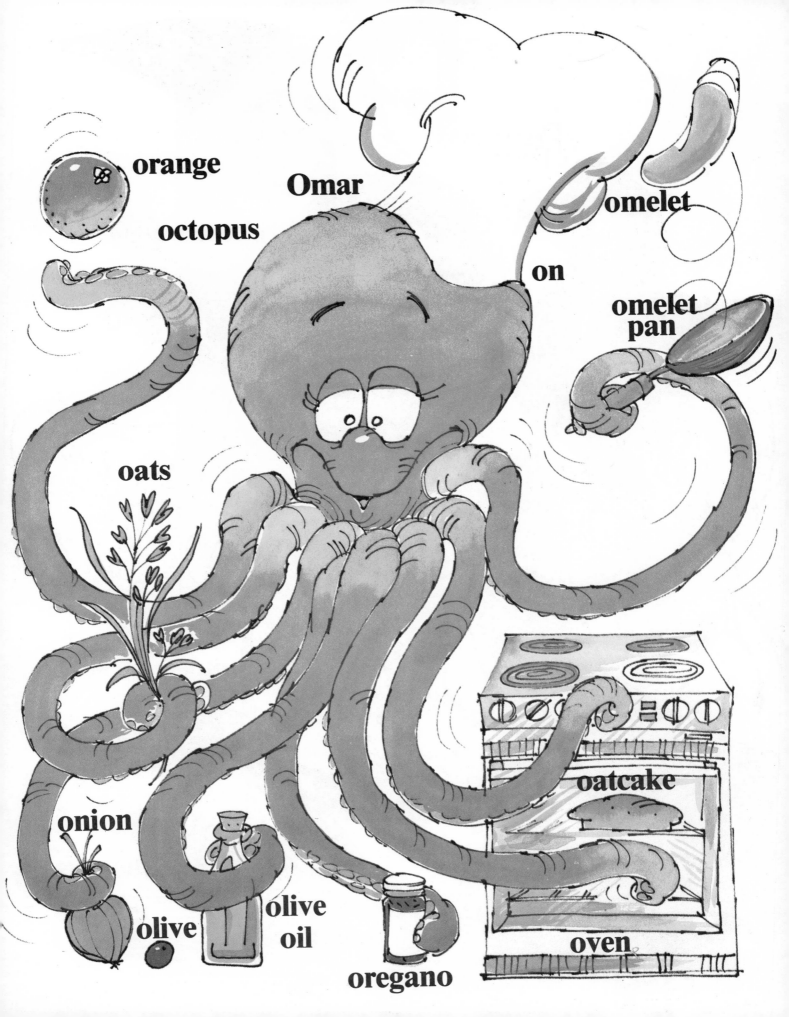

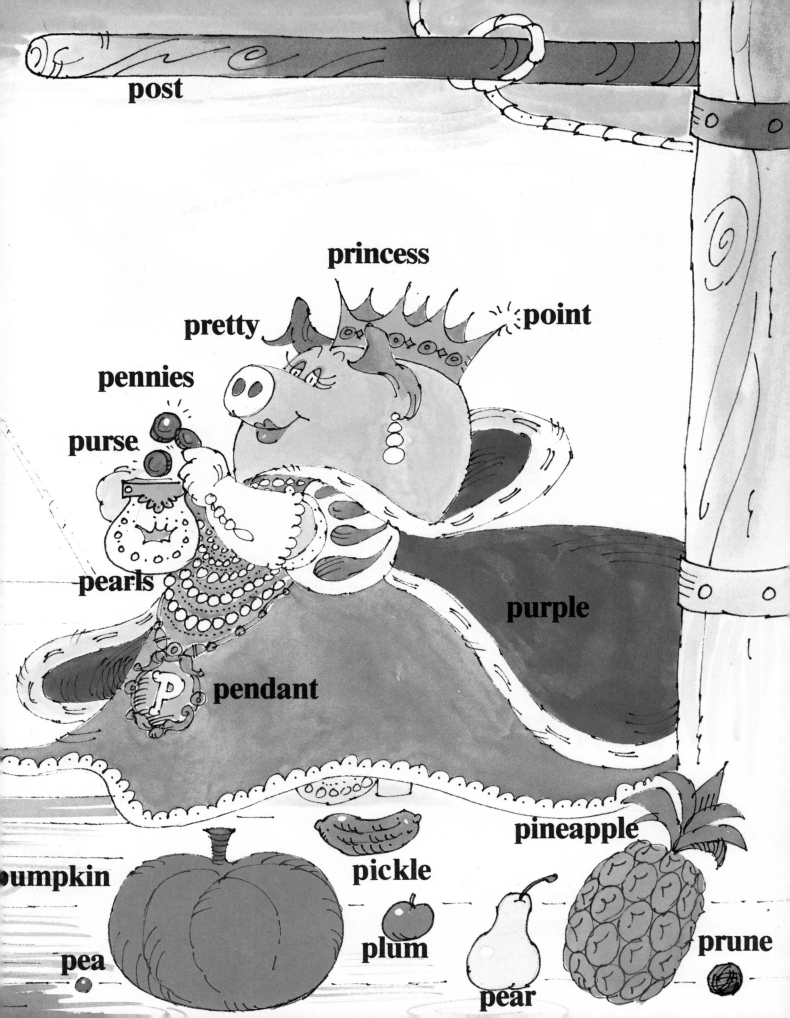

Qq

queen

queen bee

quilt

quill

quote

"To be
or not
to be.
Will S."

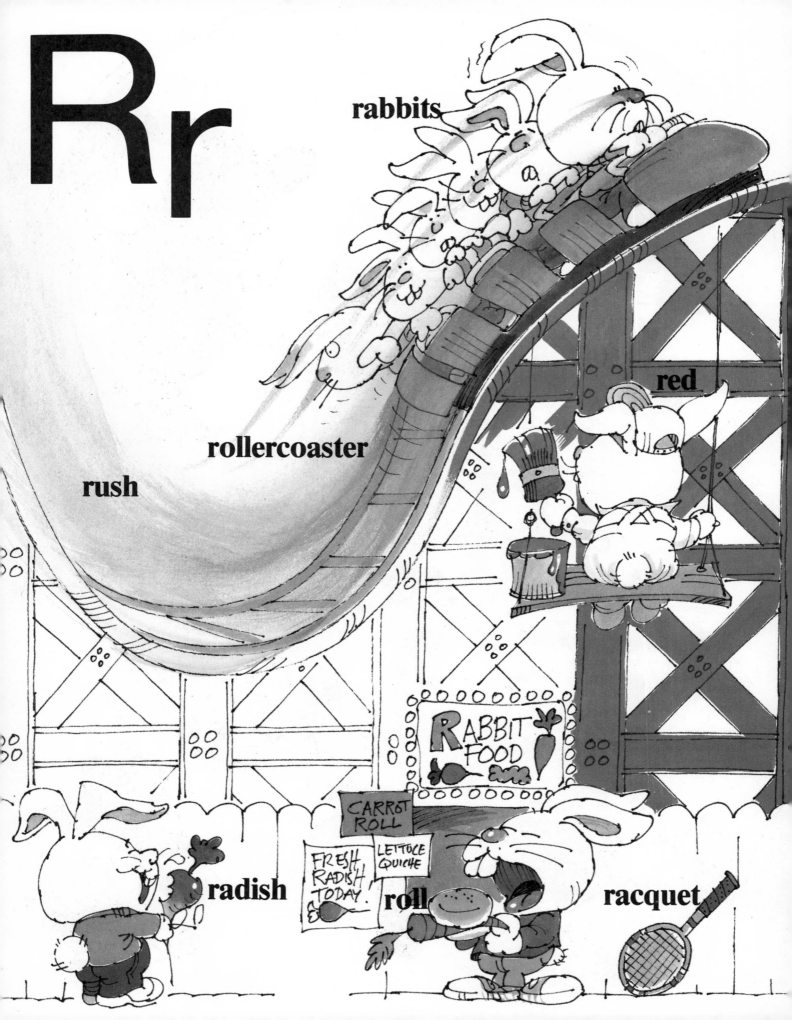

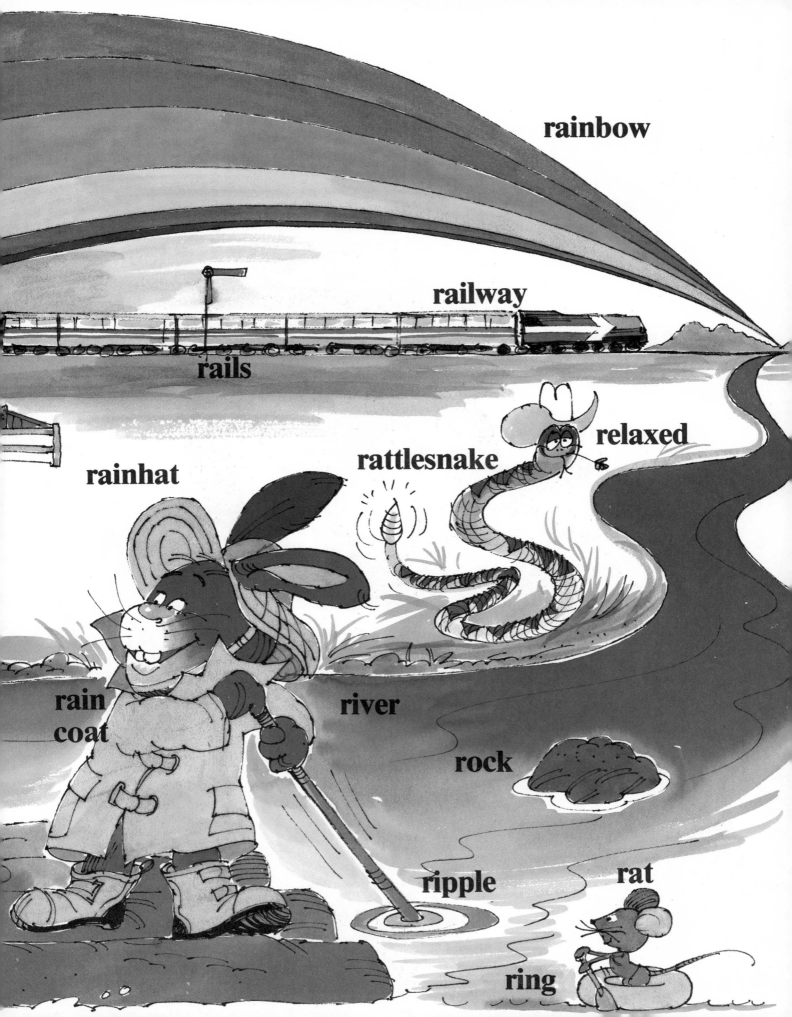

Swimming ←

sign

seat

soda

sack

shoes

Sharon

socks

sandwich

sunglasses

stripe

swim suit

sandcastle

shells

shovel

sandpiper

Sam

sunhat

sail

submarine

splash

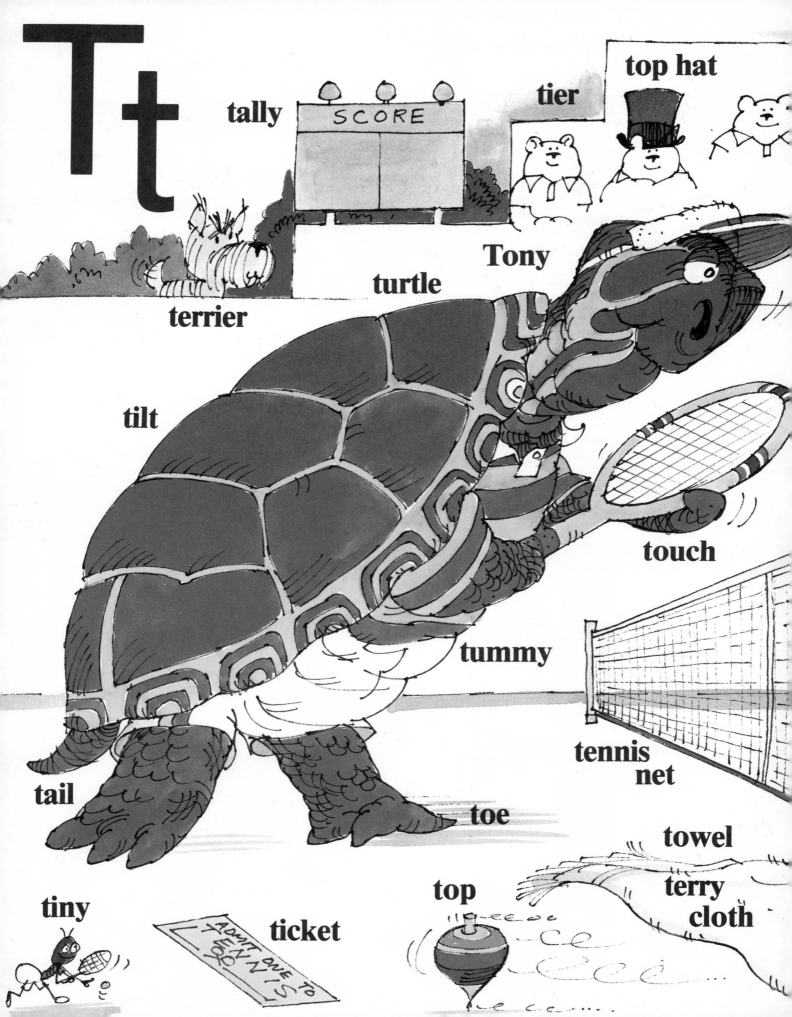

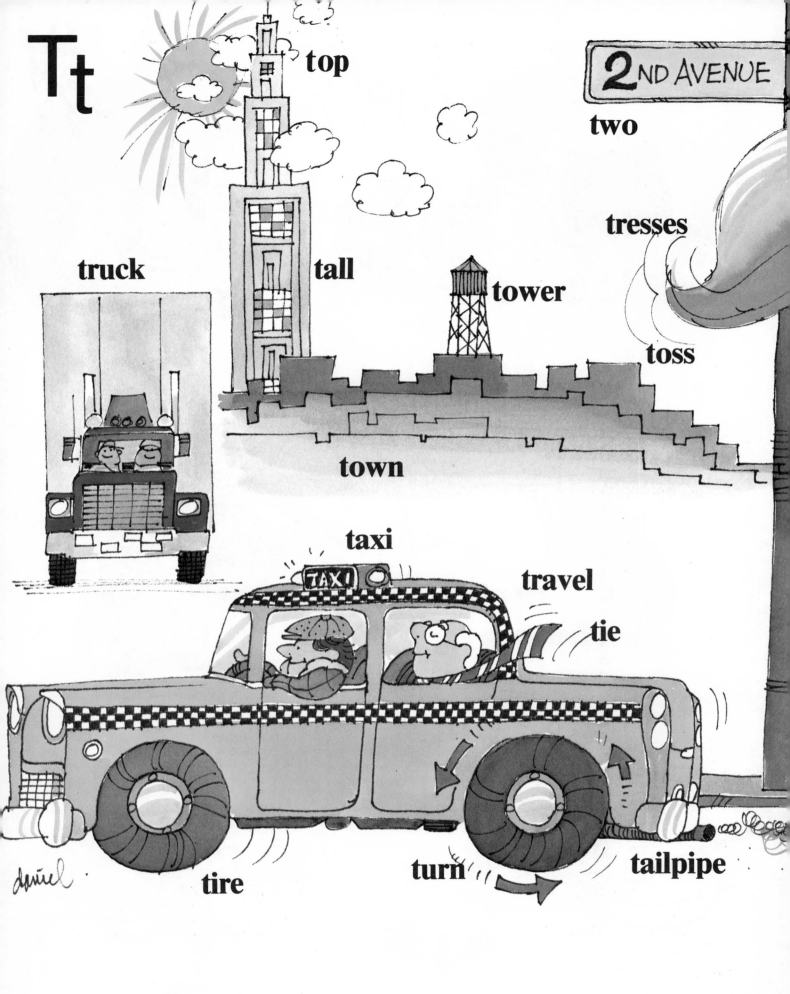

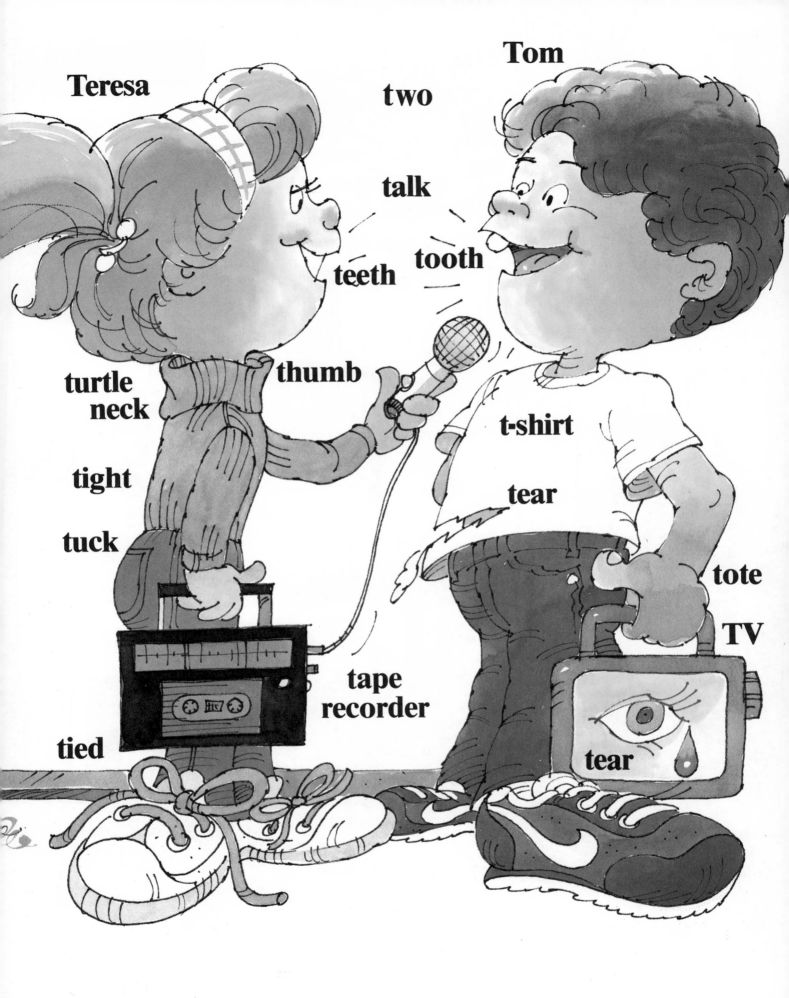

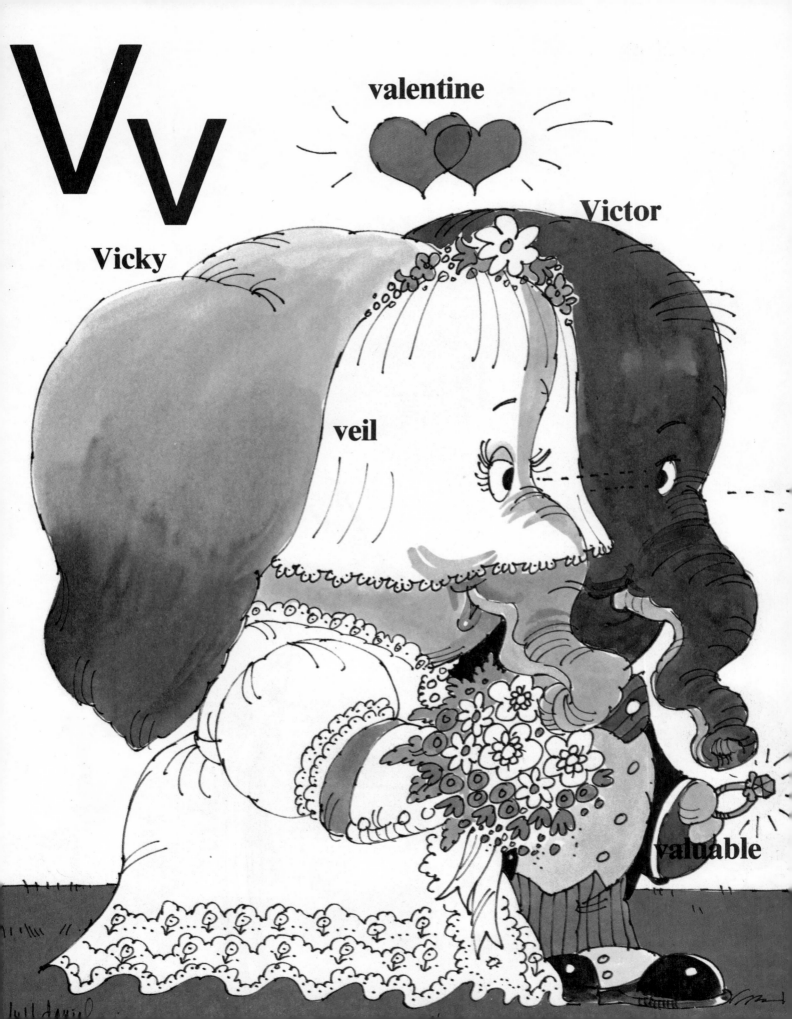

valance

Vincent

vision

voice

violet

vest

ermillion

vase

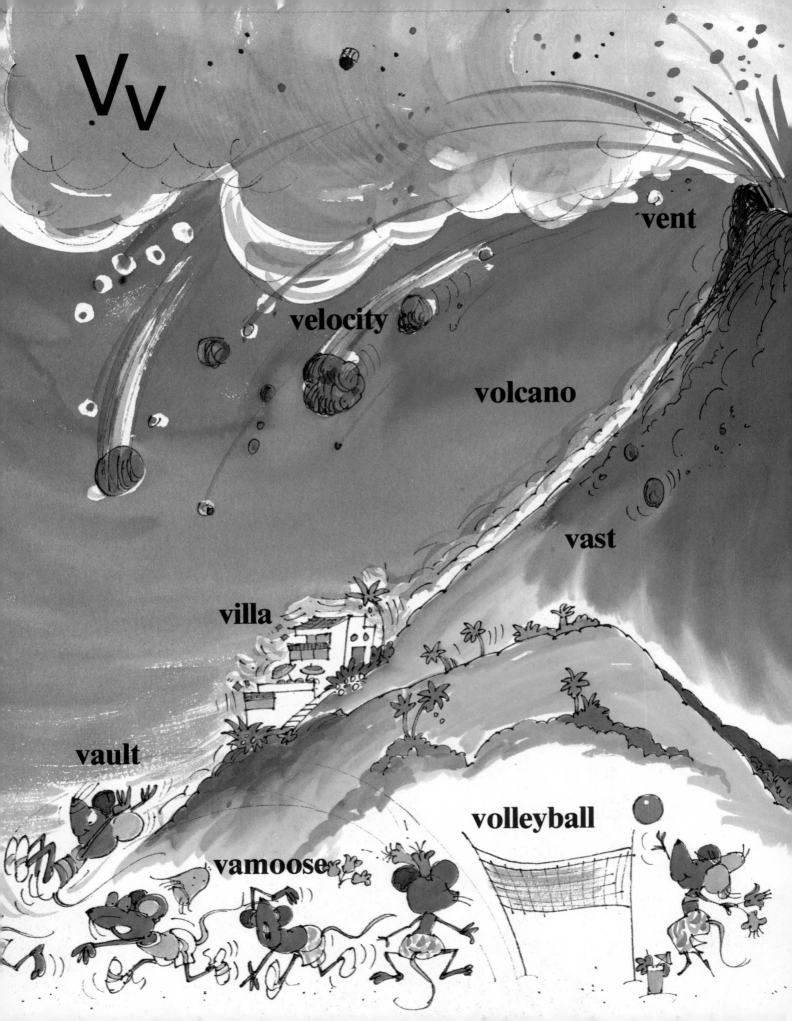

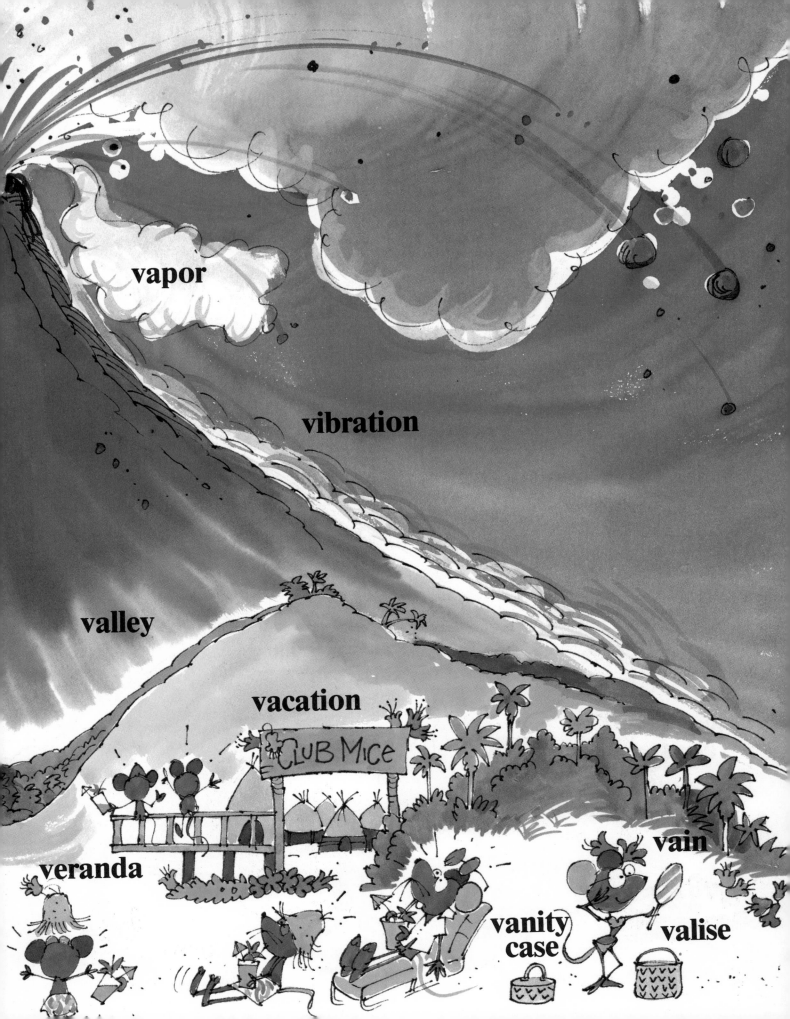

Ww

wisp

western

wall

watch

whip

wheelbarrow

wasp

waist coat

waist

wipe

wash

work

worm

wriggle

wolf

wagon

well

wheat

wing

wood

webfoot

wheel

walk

wet

water

weeds

woods

wigwam

wreath

wool

writing

workbook

wind

olen
nket

warm

woodpile

X x

Xavier

xylophone

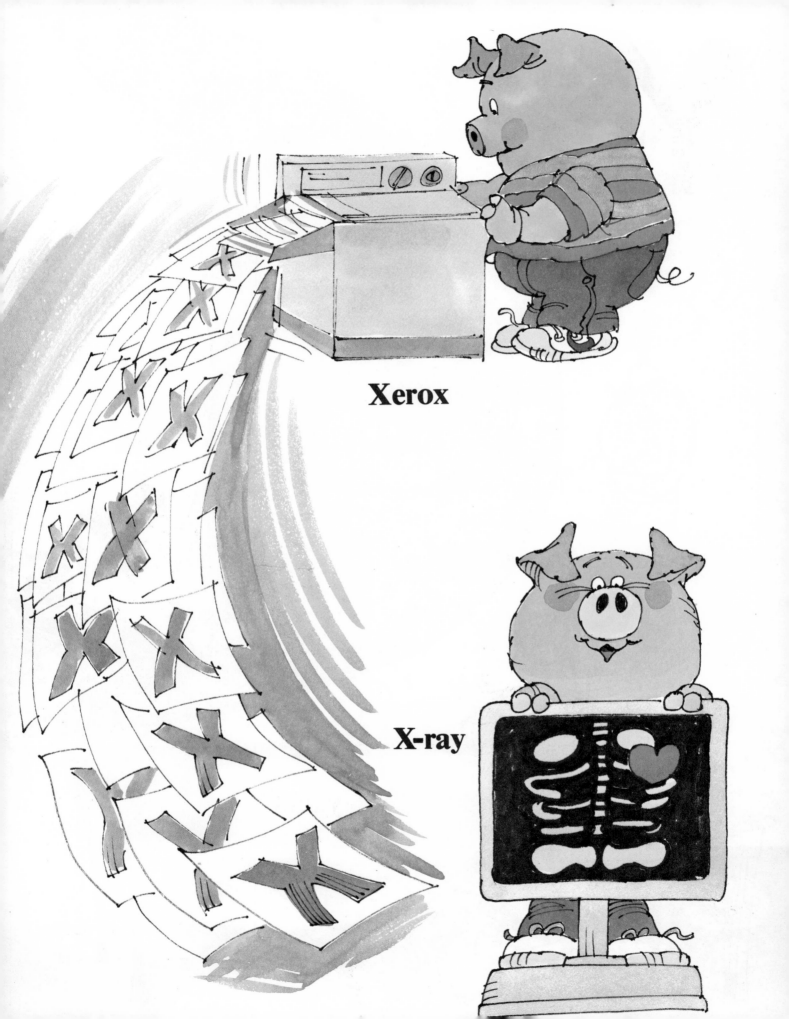

Xerox

X-ray

Yy

yell

yawl

yap

yacht

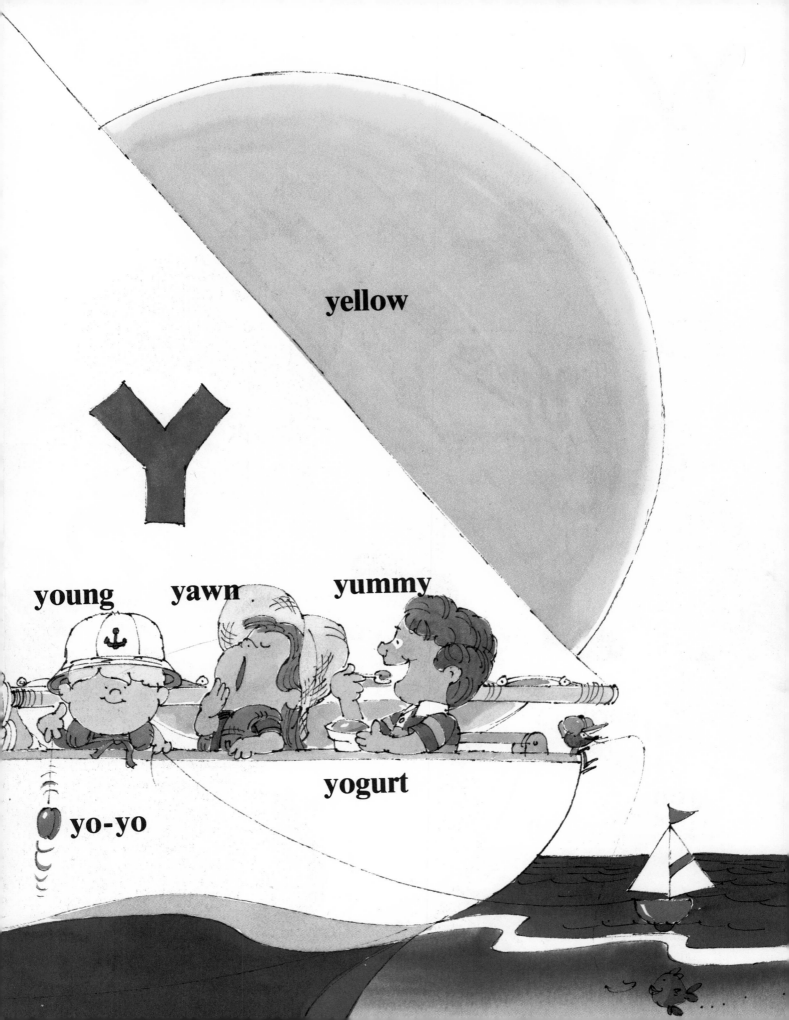

yellow

Y

young yawn yummy

yogurt

yo-yo

Yy

yankee

yak

yew

yard

yucca

you

yanks

Aa Bb Cc
Dd Ee Ff
Gg Hh
Ii Jj Kk
Ll Mm